What a Story!

Written by Paul Kropp
Illustrated by Loris Lesynski

An easy-to-read SOLO
for beginning readers

Scholastic Canada Ltd.
New York Toronto London Auckland Sydney
Mexico City New Delhi Hong Kong Buenos Aires

To Lori, my very favourite
Grade 2 teacher.
— PK

For Teresa Toten, who totally
encourages scribbling.
— LL

Text copyright © Paul Kropp 2002.
Illustrations copyright © Loris Lesynski 2002.
Cover design by Lyn Mitchell.

National Library of Canada Cataloguing in Publication Data
Kropp, Paul, 1948-
    What a story! / written by Paul Kropp ; illustrated by Loris Lesynski.

(Solo reading)
For children aged 5 and up.
ISBN 0-7791-1355-1

    I. Lesynski, Loris   II. Title.   III. Series.
PS8571.R772W43 2002   jC813'.54 C2002-901519-7   PZ7

 5 4 3 2 1   Printed and bound in Canada   02 03 04 05

Chapter 1

Sara liked her new teacher.

"My name sounds like puddle and muddle," Ms. Tuddle told the class. "But not like poodle or toodle!"

Sara liked the way Ms. Tuddle made them laugh.

But Sara didn't like the way Ms. Tuddle made them write stories.

"This month we're studying insects," Ms. Tuddle told the class. "I want all of you to imagine what it would be like to be an insect. Then write a story about it."

Chapter 2

Sara's friend Tasha said it was easy to imagine being a beetle. Her friend Lena said it was easy to write about being a butterfly.

Even George said he had fun
writing about being a spider.

But Sara couldn't get started. She couldn't imagine being an insect, so she didn't write a word.

Chapter 3

Then it was time for all the kids to read their stories. At last it was Sara's turn.

"I was going to write a story, Ms. Tuddle. But, but . . . "

Sara thought fast. "When I
turned on the computer, smoke
came out. So I called the fire
department! They put out the fire,
but the computer is a big mess.
And my dad is kind of mad."

"The fire department?" all the kids said.

"Yes. They said I was very brave. They might even give me a medal."

Sara smiled. Ms. Tuddle clapped her hands. Everyone forgot about her story.

Chapter 4

The next month, the class studied weather. Ms. Tuddle said, "I want all of you to imagine what it's like to be in a big storm. Then write a story about it."

Everybody said that would be
easy. Tasha wrote her story about
being in a hurricane. Lena wrote a
story about getting stuck outside
in a hail storm.

Even George wrote a good story about getting sucked into a tornado.

But Sara couldn't get started. She couldn't imagine herself in a big storm and so she didn't write a word.

Chapter 5

Then it was time for the kids to
read their stories. At last it was
Sara's turn.

"I was going to write a story, Ms. Tuddle. But, but . . . "

16

Sara thought fast. "I was
working at the table when my
baby brother started choking.
He was blue in the face!"

"Blue?" the kids asked.

"Yes," Sara explained. "I yelled
for my mom. Then I saw this
yellow icky thing in his mouth.
I pulled it out and threw it away.
But it landed right on top of my
story.

"Mom picked up my story with the yellow icky thing and threw them both out."

Sara looked like she would cry.
Ms. Tuddle said she understood.
Everyone forgot about her story.

Chapter 6

The next month, the whole class got ready for Valentine's Day. Ms. Tuddle said, "I want all of you to imagine being in love. Then write a story about it."

Nobody thought this would be easy, but all the kids tried hard.

Tasha wrote a story about how
her parents fell in love. Lena
wrote a story about how her
Barbie and Ken dolls fell in love.

Even George wrote a good story about two frogs who sang songs together. He sent his story to Sara in a heart-shaped envelope!

Sara didn't like any of this. She had never been in love. She didn't want to fall in love — ever — and certainly not with George. So she didn't write a word!

Chapter 7

Then it was time for all the kids to read their stories. At last it was Sara's turn.

"I was going to write a story, Ms. Tuddle. But, but . . . "

Sara thought fast. "My father wanted to look it over, but just then the phone rang and it was my dad's boss. He said Dad had to fly to London, right away. So my dad hurried to the airport because the plane was taking off, and somehow, somehow . . . "

"He took your story with him,"
George said.

"Right!" Sara agreed. "So I'm afraid I don't have my story, Ms. Tuddle."

Some of the kids laughed. Some looked at Sara. Ms. Tuddle just sighed.

Chapter 8

The next month, the class studied
the solar system. Ms. Tuddle said,
"I want all of you to imagine
being in outer space. Then write
a story about it." Ms. Tuddle
looked right at Sara.

The boys liked this outer space idea a lot.

Most of the girls thought it would be easy. Tasha wrote a story about being on Pluto and getting frozen. Lena wrote a story about getting sunburned on Mercury.

George wrote a story about
driving Sara around Mars on a
space scooter.

Chapter 9

Then it was time for all the kids to read their stories. At last it was Sara's turn.

"I was going to write a story, Ms. Tuddle. But, but . . . "

"Wait a minute!" Ms. Tuddle cried. "I love your excuses, Sara, but this time you have to write a real story — on paper. You stay in at lunch and we'll work on it together."

Chapter 10

It was quiet after all the other kids went off to lunch. Sara just had to say something!

"Well, I had the story started and then my dog chewed up the pages and . . . "

"Sara," said Ms. Tuddle.

"Well, I had it all done and
somehow it got in the toilet
and . . . "

"Sara," said Ms. Tuddle, "I had
a talk with your mom last night."

"Uh oh," Sara replied.

"Your dad never went to London," Ms. Tuddle said. "Your little brother never choked on a yellow icky thing. And your computer never caught on fire."

"No, not really." Sara's face felt very warm.

Chapter 11

"You can imagine so many things, Sara! Why do you have so much trouble writing a story?" asked Ms. Tuddle.

"I guess I can't see myself as a
bug, or on Mars, or in love," Sara
told her. "I'd rather write about
real life."

"That's a good idea," Ms. Tuddle
agreed. "I'll help you."

Chapter 12

Once Sara got started, she didn't really need much help. The words kept coming faster and faster. She wrote and wrote and wrote. She stopped only once to look up.

"Ms. Tuddle," Sara asked, "how do you spell elephant?"

Paul Kropp

I started writing stories for my grade two teacher, Mrs. Brown. Back then, most of my stories were about airplanes and bombs, because all I could draw were planes and big smudges where things exploded.

Mrs. Brown wanted me to do "nice" stories about bunnies or mice, but I couldn't draw bunnies and I was afraid of mice. I became an author anyway, mostly writing novels for older kids. I still don't write about bunnies or mice, but sometimes I'll put in an elephant.

Loris Lesynski

I've always been good at making up excuses for not getting my work done on time! That's why I understood this story so well while I was doing the illustrations.

I write stories and poems as well as drawing. Just like Sara, sometimes I freeze up when there's a WRITING ASSIGNMENT. I should get Ms. Tuddle's phone number — she sounds very encouraging.

I love the end of this story. It's great that everybody gets to have his or her own idea of what "real life" is.